Visit us on the Web!
rhcbooks.com

Educators and librarians, for a variety of teaching tools, visit us at
RHTeachersLibrarians.com

Library of Congress Cataloging-in-Publication Data is available upon request.
ISBN 978-0-593-11978-5 (trade) — ISBN 978-0-593-11979-2 (lib. bdg.) —
ISBN 978-0-593-11980-8 (ebook)

MANUFACTURED IN THE UNITED STATES OF AMERICA
10 9 8 7 6 5 4 3
First Edition

I Can Be Anything!

by Bob Staake

BEGINNER BOOKS®
A Division of Random House

This is me.

And I can be . . .
ANYthing I WANT to be!

I'm a car
on a ski.

I'm a house
in a tree!

Look at me fly!
I'm a plane WAY up high!

I'm a green-headed monster
with a giant red eye!

Look at me now!

I'm the cat's meow.

I'm a robot

on a dairy cow!

Hey there! Hi there!
Come on down!
I'm a slide that's shaped
like a birthday clown!

I'm a surfboard
for a whale!

I'm a boat
that you can sail!

Watch me change!
I'm something NEW!
A panda in the city zoo!

I'm a barn
weather vane!

I'm a train with a crane!

And JUST when
you need me—
an umbrella . . .
in the rain!

I'm a lighthouse
in a foggy cloud!

I'm a tuba honking
WAY TOO LOUD!

STADIUM

I'm the blimp you see
at football games!

I'm the art you find in picture frames!

Hey there!
Hi there!
Look at me!

There's really
NOTHING
I can't be!

I can be ANYthing!
I can be EVERYthing!

What's the thing YOU want to be?

DO IT! TRY IT!

Then you'll see.

Okay, kids!

It's time to go!

Wait, don't leave us!

No,

no,

NO!

LOOK!

I can be . . .

...a DINOSAUR!